THE
PERFECT LINE

By

Subin Park

Gold Moose Publishing books may be purchased for educational, business, or sales promotional uses. For information, please email us at hyeay@hyeay.com

ISBN: 978-1-969181-05-4

THE
PERFECT LINE

Table of Contents

Chapter 1

Canvas

Iris

I feel bad for this new generation; I mean, I guess I'm also envious of them, since they won't really know the difference between how it used to be like and the new regulations implemented now, but that's also really sad. They are basically experiments; they just won't understand how it feels to be normal, to live normal. Or perhaps it's us. We, the ones before BCI, will be the weird ones now, right? I don't know, but I definitely don't support BCI. It's great that everyone is excited about this new product, but isn't it just restricting people from their freedom and personal information? If everyone turns over all their memories to it, what will be private to them? Will anything be personal? All data or information about certain opinions or thoughts could be public to everyone, or at least to the government. Since there's even an AI that processes and answers everything, people won't have to think. They will just be fully dependent on this new technology. With BCI, everything is going to be so much duller and more lifeless, basically evolving backwards.

I remember a few years ago when BCI was first founded, it was all over the news, "Brain Computer Interface - Changing the Future". There was no one who wasn't talking about it. It's kind of funny that it started in my old university. Obviously, I did not go near the STEM buildings during my time there. I was fine in my art studio, exploring my creativity, experimenting with new oil paintings for our exhibitions. But when they invented the first version of BCI, you couldn't help knowing about it. At first, some people were skeptical, because how could anyone trust giving up their information to a computer? But as it continued to develop and more funds went into researching it, people seemed to have a shift in perspective. Suddenly, everything about BCI became *so* great and now everyone is looking forward to when BCI will begin to be administered.

As much as I don't like digging into techy things, I think BCI is common knowledge now. But I still don't know if it's good to connect people's brains to computers. So many people have tried to convince me, highlighting all of its benefits. I always say, "That's a great point" or something along the lines of that and agree with them, but deep down I really don't. It's horrible what they are doing, and I know this isn't going to end well, but mostly everyone is inclined for this to be fully embraced. That's why I'm not disagreeing or causing any controversies, especially as an art student, people would just not care or just criticize and shut me down for anything I say. So, I'm keeping quiet. But I really wished someone would go out there and challenge this idea. There have been thousands of groups resisting other changes: why not this one?

Maybe I am too old for this. I am too old for this. I remember getting extremely annoyed at my parents for not being able to work with computers properly, so maybe I just don't understand this, it's just a generation gap. I'm too behind. But still, something that's really weird is how this isn't optional. Shouldn't it be that people who want to participate and know more about themselves and potentially get all of their personal information taken away follow them like a clueless duck, while people who actually think about consequences get to just stay back, I mean where did all my freedom go?

So, I asked Sarah if we could meet up. As a well-regarded computer engineer for a high-end company, she's always incredibly busy, people usually schedule around two months ahead just to get a meeting with her. But she'll usually make time for me if I ask. It's probably because the first time we met, she was extremely shy. I think we were in 2nd grade, and she did not talk to anyone. A lot of people thought she was weird, and she kind of was, but honestly, she could do so many cool things, like solving a Rubix cube or those word crosses in the back of newspapers. Once, she looked really bored all by herself in the cafeteria, so I sat with her at lunch. I remember her face specifically, brightening up as I asked whether I could sit with her, I knew then that we would become best friends.

We are also complete opposites. She's the prodigy, every parent's dream child. I swear she can do anything she puts her mind to, except for art, so I'm glad I have the upper hand for one thing. But she speaks five languages fluently: English, Mandarin, French, German, and Spanish, skipped 3 grades, got into all the Ivy Leagues, has a PhD in engineering, plays three instruments and so much more, but she's still my best friend. I mean there's no reason not to be, she's so kind and patient and helps me with everything. She's the only reason I passed the subjects that I was forced to take during Highschool.

"Hey Sarah! How are you? Wow, it's been a while since we last talked, but can I ask you something really quickly?"

"Hi Iris, I'm doing great. Sure, what do you want to ask? Is it another essay proposal for your new art exhibition?" She replied with a slight smirk.

"Oh yeah, I forgot about that," I do need to work on that if I want to get the deal sorted out. "Well, I need help with that for sure, but also what do you think about BCI, genuinely curious you know?"

"You? Talking about modern technology? Woah, never seen this side of Iris before. But BCI, I love it. It's crazy, you know, the amount of work they put in. Do you get how impossible this idea was? It's like trying to invent a new colour. You can't, because every colour possible is already found, that's what you think, or what the world thinks, until someone breaks the barriers to find it. The fact that someone found a new element was already crazy, but using that to create new technology, in just a decade, I swear people are getting so much smarter. And don't even get me started on the code, compressing the code to fit all the lines into…"

Boring. Maybe I shouldn't have asked her about this. I don't know why I thought she would think the same as me. I liked her analogy about colours though, one point to BCI I guess.

"You good? You look like you zoned out right there." Sarah waited, looking at me with concern.

"Oh sorry, my bad. This is pretty interesting, I really loved your analogy. Um, wait, just to get this straight, you love BCI right?"

"Of course! Who wouldn't? It's going to change our future and I'm so excited! Especially for engineering. BCI is going to give me so much more information about what people genuinely need and I can build machines and robots in correlation to those thoughts. Obviously, this translates to many industries right now. For example, psychology is going to have it so much easier now that most of the data that they couldn't ever efficiently or ethically source is in their hands, they can find all sorts of associations and who knows how much that is going to help us. Since BCI also comes with our own AI, everyone is going to be much healthier and probably just happier overall!" Sarah smiled. "So, what do you think about it?"

"Me?" I realized all this time, no one has really ever asked me, except for myself. But Sarah was sincere, she actually wanted to know how I felt. But what did I think about it? I don't like it right? That's what I've been telling myself. And anyway, I can't like it, it's terrifying, all the possibilities of humans just becoming brain-dead zombies, but I can't tell her that. Even though I've told her every single one of my secrets, I'm not sure about this one. What if she tells someone, and everyone will be against me. Everyone would think I'm weird and that I'm crazy, delusional. I have to lie, just for now, until someone else stands up. "I love BCI too! Still not exactly sure on how it works, but I also think it's going to be extremely beneficial!"

"Glad you think that way too! Wanna go get coffee or something? Wait, I'm kind of hungry, I want a sandwich. There's a new bagel place downtown if you want to go there?"

"Sure, that sounds great."

We arrived at the bagel place, catching up on a lot. But no matter how much I tried to steer the conversation out of it, BCI kept creeping its way in, like it was manipulating and controlling our conversation, like those annoying viruses that keep pestering us. After Sarah ordered her ham and cheese sandwich and I ordered a classic cream cheese bagel, Sarah continued her raving about BCI. Honestly, I couldn't deny all the benefits she described, but I couldn't help but feel a knot in my stomach.

Chapter 2

Wire

Sarah

I have been pretty busy lately, writing research papers, finding relevant data, and most importantly figuring out how to use BCI in research. But I've been neglecting my social relationships, I haven't talked to my parents in so long and I'm sure my co-workers think I'm a workaholic. I might be, but that's just because I love working. I get to use all of my brain power thinking and solving a single problem, every other nonsensical problem that the world throws at me disappears. I also get a lot of money out of it, so I don't really care about what other people think of me. Sometimes I don't understand why Iris still likes me, she always sends me texts, checking up on me from time to time. I usually ghost her or when I do read her messages, I reply extremely dryly, even though I know it, I just can't help it. But she did ask to meet, and it was actually pretty nice to take a break from my never-ending research. I liked being able to talk rave about all the wonders of BCI and have someone who actually cared to listen.

After hanging out with her though, I can't help but notice how strange she was. It's been a while since we met in real life. Usually, I'm helping her write her bio or artist's statements for her artworks, which is a nice change of topics from math and engineering. But she's different now, or at least from what I remember. She's still a wonderful listener, but she started zoning out when I was talking about BCI in a way I've never seen her do before. She feels so disconnected. Maybe BCI isn't as interesting of a topic for her, but I wonder if something's happening. I don't have time to think about her anyways. I can't work on my own problems and hers anymore, short essays to help her get deals, sure, they are pretty easy, but whatever she thinks about BCI is her own problem.

Chapter 3

Notebook

Iris

I pulled out my notebook to sketch. I tried something simple, just a person. But my page looked different today, it was darker, smudged, messier, was the person crying?

I turned on the holovision, and the screen lit up the room. I had turned off the lights to save on my energy bills. (Annoying how they are making us pay for energy that is renewable, just because they have full control over it). I put on the news because I don't like the reality shows that are actually just hurting people mentally or physically. Don't even get me started on the children's shows that are definitely not meant for them to watch. And then I saw it, the news I had been dreading: BCI is globally approved, countries are now mandated to allocate citizens a number for the BCI test. I checked my phone. No new messages. Maybe they forgot about me. I mean I barely contribute to this society anyways, maybe someone erased my name, or maybe I can get Sarah to erase it for me. No, but then she'll realize, but maybe she should realize, she could help me navigate this mess, but no one will understand what I'm going through. Everyone would just think I'm crazy, but I'm not, I swear I'm not. I don't even know if you believe me.

My phone lit up, were my hands shaking? I turned my phone on, it had a message, "Number 413,890,542", okay that's not too bad, actually that's pretty good, they probably can only get through around a hundred people per day. My math isn't good, but I'm sure I have a lot of time before I have to take the test, "Please arrive at the Lopisis Research Center 796451 on the 13th of October at 2:30 pm sharp". Wait the 13th? There's no way, that's in a week, I think. How are they going through so many people? This isn't possible right?

Chapter 4

Phone

Sarah

I paced around my room, trying to figure out what would be the best way to pitch this new big idea when I got a message from my phone. My phone is usually on silent except for business related or urgent notifications so I was kind of surprised I had received something that had come through this late into the night. I opened my phone, and I saw a message. From the government? Oh. It read, "Please arrive at the Lopisis Research Center 796451 on the 16th of October at 7:00 am sharp". Interesting. I swapped to the news screen. Okay, now it makes more sense, BCI is finally being implemented. I'm pretty excited to learn more about how it works and how I work too, just more about myself in general.

Okay, so let's go back to what I was doing, yes, the pitch. I tried to get back to work, forcing work upon myself, but I couldn't focus. I kept thinking of Iris, I'm not sure why it was distracting me, but I wondered if she had gotten her BCI appointment yet, so I called her.

"Sarah?" There was a slight hesitation in her voice.

"Hi Iris, I just got my date for BCI, what about you?" I asked

"Oh yeah, I got mine, 13th of October, surprised that it's in a week. Didn't know they were so efficient with this." Iris replied.

"Mhm, mine is on the 16th of October."

"That's so fun, we are basically doing the test on the same day!" Something was off, her words were happy, definitely, but her voice wasn't. I don't know, maybe it was her tone, something was wrong, her voice didn't match what she was saying.

"Yeah."

"So is that all you wanted to talk about?" Iris asked.

"Oh, well I just wanted to know how you feel about it, you know."

"Feel about it? Great, I guess. Finally doing something productive with my time you know." Iris said, letting out a small chuckle at the end.

"That's good, I'm excited too! I'll talk to you soon about it, I have to go work on a pitch right now."

"Woah, at 4 am? Well good luck with that! And good night if you do get sleep."

"Good night to you too, sorry for waking you up."

"No worries, I woke up from the message anyways. But thanks, I'll talk to you soon."

That was a normal conversation, she didn't say anything wrong or weird, but why do I still have this knot in my stomach? I know something is wrong with her.

Chapter 5

Mirror

Iris

Sarah called me?

We've been friends for years, and I just recently realized how I've always been the clingy one, probably because no one really liked me, but still. She has never reached out to me first, it was always me, so why the sudden change of heart? I answered the phone.

"Sarah?" I didn't know what to feel, was this good news? Bad news? I don't know, I just don't.

"Hi Iris, I just got my date for BCI, what about you?" Oh, I calmed myself, realizing how tense I was. Nothing was wrong, she just wanted to know about BCI, classic Sarah.

"Oh yeah, I got mine, 13th of October, surprised that it's in a week. Didn't know they were so efficient with this." I replied.

"Mhm, mine is on the 16th of October." Oh, she's after me, so I can't even ask her how it was, well, gotta keep this conversation moving.

"That's so fun, we are basically doing the test on the same day"

"Yeah." What was that dry reply, does she know I don't like BCI? Was I too obvious? No way, okay maybe I should be a bit more cautious. Or maybe this is just her normal self, dry as always, I'm just always over analyzing things.

"So, is that all you wanted to talk about?" I asked.

"Oh, well I just wanted to know how you feel about it, you know."

"Feel about it?" Wait, okay calm down, she's probably just making small talk, continue the conversation and it will be fine. "Oh, great, I guess. Finally doing something productive with my time you know."

"That's good, I'm excited too! I'll talk to you soon about it, I have to go work on a pitch right now."

"Woah, at 4 am? Well good luck with that! And good night if you do get sleep."

"Good night to you too, sorry for waking you up."

"No worries, I woke up from the message anyways. But thanks, I'll talk to you soon."

I ended the call. Me. I'm so confused, what's happening? Sarah called me and I ended it. Maybe she knows I don't like BCI. What if she tells the government, what if I'm now imprisoned forever? For going against what everyone thinks. I have to prove to her I'm normal, I'm normal...

Chapter 6

Smiles

Iris

I could tell after the first group of people got their BCI test done, everyone looked so much happier, too happy. A lot of people shouldn't have gotten their BCI test done yet, but there was no one out here that was ungroomed or not smiling like me. They all looked superhuman, easily getting from one place to another and basically knowing how to solve every problem that they face. It seemed kind of nice, I wouldn't need to trouble myself by thinking anymore, but would we even have to work anymore? What would be the point of living?

Suddenly someone looked at me, stared at me. Was it my hood? My dark clothes? Or maybe because I wasn't smiling like everyone else? They came towards me, closer and closer, not breaking eye contact for a second. I wanted to look away, but I couldn't. Their face started morphing, a guy, a girl? I couldn't tell. Some kind of darkness erased their face as if they were just a drawing in someone's sketchbook, leaving behind only a white smile. Weird posture, weird something, I couldn't put my mind on it, it put its arm towards me like it was trying to take my soul away. Maybe it can read my mind. Does it know my true feelings about BCI?. Wait, I can't let them know though, but how am I supposed to beat artificial intelligence? How can I be one step ahead of a supercomputer? I needed help, I really did. I looked around, everywhere, but they were all the same. Scribbled faces, weird stances, staring at me with a white smile. They were all looking at me. Why? Why were they smiling? Why were they looking at me? Their smiles got bigger, but they didn't look happy. They all came closer, circling me. I had nowhere to run.

Chapter 7

Hand

Sarah

Recently, I've been assigned less work, more time for me, I guess. But I didn't know what to do. My online buddy suggested that I take a walk, which is beneficial physically and especially mentally for me. So, I did.

Sometimes I honestly forget how beautiful it is outside. I remember when we made roads with asphalt, and what were those things? Just cars, right? I mean the government is doing a great job, so many more trees and the buildings looked like they were piercing holes in the sky. I forgot how nice it was to breathe the city air, so clean, and everything finally felt so peaceful. The only problem is trying to navigate this labyrinth, I always get the timing wrong for getting on the holo-stairs and I end up waiting 2 minutes for it to come back. I guess that's why I'm excited for BCI, everything would just be much more convenient.

Off the corner of my eye, I saw a commotion. You don't see that often. I don't like being a part of big drama,

I would prefer staying out of it. I was going to walk away, thank God I didn't, but I saw her, Iris, in the middle of the circle. Crying? I ran over, pushing through people, but the crowd felt endless. I finally got to the middle, everyone was asking if she was okay, some were saying she was crazy. Her hair was frizzy, messed up; she looked pale; her whole body was shaking; she had dark circles under her eyes, like she hadn't slept in days. I pulled her out, ignoring all the stares and people calling us weird. I took us to whatever café was closest and got both of us a nice chocolate cake and a cookie to share, hoping to calm Iris down.

Chapter 8

Café

Iris

Somehow, I was in a cafe, eating. Sarah, eating too. The café was bustling with people, all chatting happily to friends and family. We were not talking. Finally, Sarah broke the quiet.

"So, you want to explain what happened over there?"

Ugh, I'll eat, hopefully she'll change the topic.

"Are you good? I mean you looked pretty scared. Not gonna lie, you still do." She continued.

"Huh?" I reply, stuffing my mouth with delicious chocolate goods, I should come here more often.

"Stop!"

I looked up at her.

"What's wrong with you? I just saved you from whatever you were doing over there, and you won't even explain to me? Just stuffing your mouth with this stupid baked stuff. I genuinely don't know what happened to you because you clearly aren't talking to me, but I can't communicate with you if this is a one-sided conversation, it's not how it works. Just talk to me, please."

"I don't know. I really don't. What happened?"

"I can't with you!" She got up, picked up her phone. "I'm just trying to help you, but clearly you don't want any help. I'm just going to leave now. You finish that and just do whatever you want. And don't even bother thanking me." She stormed out through the doors and crossed the road.

I finally got home. I looked at a blank canvas propped against the wall. I could title this, "My mind when you talked to me" and give it to Sarah. Ugh, why can't I remember anything? It's fine, I just need to sketch, let myself out.

Chapter 9

Iris

The canvas is still blank.

Chapter 10

Promise

Iris

I walked through the sliding glass doors, into the bright marbled room. As soon as I entered, a nurse guided me.

"Oh, hello. I'm here for the BCI test, I'm –"

"Don't bother with names, I would have too many to memorize anyways. Just give me your number and let me lead you to your room"

"Okay, um can I check my phone for my number, I forgot."

"Can you please hurry up; we have to get through a lot of people you know?"

"Oh yeah, sorry, give me a moment." I searched through my text messages, it honestly didn't take that long to find it, no one messages me anyways, but what if I didn't tell her my number. What if I said 'oops, came on the wrong date' and just left. She didn't know my number; she didn't know I had to be here today. She's in a rush, she probably doesn't care if I just leave, right?

"Hello? I'm really sorry, but I don't have the time to take care of your unpreparedness. Would you like me to search your name on our database?"

Oh, I guess they would know if I didn't come then. Their annoying database probably alerts them if someone doesn't come, not like someone wouldn't because BCI is everyone's dream. "Sorry, my number is 413890542."

"Okay, and you're in. Please follow me into room 83."

The place was packed with people, which makes sense if they want to go through over a few hundred thousand people per day, but still the place was pretty clean: white marble and polished floors, ironed couches, and the chandelier was beautiful.

"And you are here, your doctor will tell you everything you need to know. Goodbye!" That excitement was definitely forced.

"Hello! I'm Doctor Maques, but please just call me doctor, I don't really have much time around here. I'm sure you know what BCI is, but let me explain a bit deeper, you know, just giving you the details on how it would work. So please, sit down on the chair, I'll explain as we continue."

I sat down, guess I'm doing this now. I could just run out, the door isn't locked and the doctor is the only other person in this room. But he's probably much stronger than me, and what would I even do? Just run away and hide forever, they'd probably find me even in some other country since everyone just loves BCI, like those bugs blindly flying towards the light, but I have to accept my fate now, humanity's fate.

He started placing wires with metallic tape on the end to various parts of my body, mostly near my head. "So these wires will connect you to the computer which can hold up to 1 yottabyte of data. The extraction will take around 20 minutes to complete. Once your information is extracted (don't worry you still keep it, we just make another copy in our computer) the computer will start processing it and this takes about 3 minutes. Once fully processed, the computer creates its own artificial intelligence, suitable to you, customized to however your brain has already developed, even the parts you're not aware of. It will be the most compatible AI possible, matching every single one of your personality traits and hobbies perfectly. It will help navigate you through the fastest routes, help you easily gain information, and whatever else you have to do. Some caution is that it may hurt your eyes a bit since we are implanting a technological cell into your eye that will help you visualize the information that your personal artificial intelligence will send you. We'll plant another cell into your ear so you can hear them. We do require you to stay awake and try to have the least amount of thoughts you can. Thank you, I will leave you to it, just stay still and see you in 30 minutes!"

He left. I would leave too, but it feels like a lot of weight is physically pushing me down on this seat. Don't have thoughts, don't have thoughts, don't have thoughts. Yeah, that's impossible. Well it doesn't hurt, the metal tape is cooling on my bare skin. The tape on my head feels kind of heavy though. It's starting to tingle a bit. What will happen once they learn I don't want BCI? Will the robot or whatever that matches me perfectly, agree with me? My body is starting to ache, especially around the tape, I don't really know how to describe it. My head is definitely hurting, but I know I have to stay awake. I can do that. The clock looks like it isn't ticking anymore. The aching has become pain. My whole body hurts. How can everyone look so happy if they went through this much pain? I didn't think it could get worse, but it's starting to. I'm not sure how much longer I can keep myself awake. If I die now at least I'll know I died without getting BCI. That's not too bad–

Chapter 11

Screen

Iris

"Hello Ms. Calloway. Thank you for your participation. I hope you are feeling great after doing your BCI test, excited to see you around soon!"

"Sorry?" The floor was still clean and marbled. I was laying on a sofa with gorgeous floral patterns and the room was bright, extremely bright.

"My apologies, you have completed your participation requirement for BCI. Currently you may be confused or disorientated, but don't worry your memories should return in around 5 minutes. You can wait outside for that. Some aftereffects we have noticed are slight headaches, but those should be fixed if you take one of the pills available outside. Once again, thank you for your participation. The door is right there."

"What did I participate in?" I tried to get up, but my back was sore, and my legs felt like jelly. I felt lightheaded, but how kind of her to offer pills to me.

"The information center is outside. Once you go there, they will answer every question you have!"

"Okay, thank you so much!" It took a while, but when I got to the door, the coolness of the bronze handle sent shivers all over my body. Outside the door the white marble floor led up to an enormous room with a chandelier hanging from the ceiling. Everything was nicely polished, and the information center was right in front of me. Everything felt and looked so exceptionally nice.

"Hi, could you explain what happened to me? Where am I?"

"Hello, you just completed your BCI test! I've only been tasked to give you pills for your headache so I apologize if I can't be of much service for your queries."

"Sorry, could you clarify where I am?"

"As I mentioned, I have been tasked to give you your pills. I have no idea what has happened, but please soon, other participants of BCI are also waiting."

"What is the date today?"

"Today is the 13th of October, please take the pills and leave."

I took the pill. Back out on the street, with trees growing in their planters under the bright blue skies with cotton candy shaped clouds. My artificial intelligence's name was Aiza, and she helped me get home through all the complicated traffic of people.

Chapter 12

Light

Sarah

Iris certainly has been cheerful since her BCI appointment. I want to be happy for her, and I am. I mean, I feel great for her, she finally moved on from her pessimistic, depressed era, but something about her happiness is unsettling. I've never seen her like *this* before. But isn't happiness always a good thing?

"Hi Sarah!" She waved at me from in front of the coffee shop, all dressed up and cleaned up, definitely haven't ever seen her act this way.

"Hi Iris. How are you?"

"I'm great! I'm so excited for the coffee here because I heard that it was absolutely delicious! I'm sure it would be perfect for you. Thanks so much for accepting my invitation to meet up!"

"You're welcome? Okay let's go in and order." Her speech felt a bit more polished, I guess.

"Sure!"

The inside of the cafe was pretty nice; the walls were consumed by intricate patterns filled with floral designs and windows that let in a lot of sunlight. As one of the last people doing the BCI test, I get to really observe how everything is slowly changing. She told me to sit down as she ordered drinks and pastries for us to share. Even the table had a lovely tablecloth with gold details around the edges, same for the cushions on the chairs we sat on.

Iris chatted about everything: the coffee beans, lightning, and the artworks hung throughout the cafe. I kept expecting her to complain about the heat, how crowded it was, or especially about the prices of all the food since she's usually really stingy about that. But she didn't. Is this what happiness is supposed to look like? Being able to be blind to the world's flaws and annoyances? If so, why did it feel like something is switched off rather than on?

I looked at her face, and she smiled, but as if it was printed on.

Chapter 13

Line

Iris

"Good morning," Aiza said, soothing as ever.

"Aiza?"

"Yes, that's me. Let's go get ready now."

I got up, it was kind of nice. I felt refreshed, energetic, and excited to get out of bed. But it felt weird, too perfect.

I went to my designated art room, sat alone, not really since Aiza was also here technically. I grabbed a sketchbook and opened it, wanting to draw in it, kind of like a final placebo to find comfort in my old self, before BCI. The lines came out exactly as I wanted them on my first try. So much lovelier than those messy pages I've seen in my old sketch books, filled to the brim with messed-up sketch lines. Everything just as I want it to be.

But halfway through the perfect and precise lines, something slipped. Pressing hard with the pencil, the paper tore as a line cut across the drawing, and multiple more, messy, dark, not beautiful, ugly, but human.

For a second, I took a moment to just stare, at the flaw spreading across perfection, alive in its imperfections.

Chapter 14

Between the Lines

Sarah

I sat cross-legged on the edge of the bed, watching Iris flip silently through a sketchbook. The room was quiet except for the soft scrape of paper.

Iris used to fill silence with restless tapping, humming, and complaints about the world. Now she just smiled.

"You look…peaceful," I said, trying to sound light.

Iris looked up. "I am peaceful. Everything's perfect now."

The words should have comforted me, I think, but instead my stomach twisted. Her voice was steady, her smile flawless, her eyes steady on mine, but there was something distant about it, as if she was looking at me from far, far away.

I peeked at the notebook on her lap. As she flipped, I saw pages filled with clean, symmetrical patterns: a strange, mechanical beauty. But on the very last page, at the corner,

I caught a glimpse of a mess of black lines, almost tearing through the paper.

I started to ask her about it, but she closed the book with a soft thud before I could even open my mouth.

"Don't worry," Iris said gently. "Everything's fine."

I forced a smile back.

My phone pinged, a reminder for my BCI appointment tomorrow.

About the Author

Subin Park is a writer from Korea
who grew up in Singapore,
witnessing major technological innovations.
The Perfect Line is her debut work, illustrating
the intersections between humanity and technology
and reflecting on friendship, control, and the remains
when perfection replaces imperfection.